MIRROR OF LUST BOOK 2
A JESSICA SMITH THRILLER, MYSTERY, SUSPENSE

AVA S. KING

LATEST RELEASES: AVA S. KING

Agent Red Fatal Memory Teagan Stone Book 1
Agent Red Fatal Target Teagan Stone Book 2
Agent Red Fatal Crime Teagan Stone Book 3
Agent Red Fatal Justice Teagan Stone Book 4
Agent Red Fatal Enemy Teagan Stone Book 5
Mirror of Lies -A Jessica Smith Book 1
Agent Red Fatal Death Teagan Stone Book 6
Mirror of Lust -A Jessica Smith Book 2
Upcoming Releases (2022/2023)
Agent Red Fatal Revenge Teagan Stone Book 7
Christina Harris Mystery/Thriller Series
Agent Red Fatal Pursuit Teagan Stone Book 8
Agent Red Fatal Attack Teagan Stone Book 9

DISCLAIMER

This work of fiction contains strong language, violence and explicit content and is only intended for mature readers. The story may contain unconventional situations, language, and sexual encounters that may offend some readers. This book is for mature readers (18+).

INTRODUCTION

Sign up to Ava S. King's mailing list for news, new releases, and special offers.

www.authoravasking.com

SYNOPSIS

Jessica did her part to solve her friend's murder but knows that's only the beginning. Somewhere out there is a copycat killer who is actively searching for their next victim.

As an analyst, she's the perfect person for local police to have on their team. But those analytical skills won't help ease the pain she feels when another friend of hers is murdered.

Jessica must do everything she can to find out who's behind the disturbing crimes.

CHAPTER 1

At work, Marnie munched on the freshly washed apple while she browsed through her phone. She's back home at the hospital after being out of town and was ready to stay put. Jessica and Lainey wanted to stay in touch with each other after learning about Allison's death. Seeing as Lainey was still in Townsend, and things were still fresh after Connor and his family's news, it would be extremely hard to do that. As a nurse, she enjoyed working at Community Hospital of New York, because it allowed her to set her own schedule and travel.

"Marnie, did you check on Ruben for the night?" Another nurse on her floor sat next to her and filled out patients' charts.

"Bianca, you asked me that ten minutes ago." Marnie rolled her eyes and bit the apple one more time. Bianca Moore was around the same age as Marnie. She came to work at the hospital two years ago before Marnie went out on a few field assignments.

"Well, you know Old Lady Charlotte will come down

here to check," Bianca huffed and signed her name on the medication chart.

"Don't remind me." Marnie dumped the last remnants of the apple in the trash.

"What are you doing for the night?"

Bianca slid the bottle of lotion over and squirted a dab in her hand.

"Nothing. Going home to sleep." Marnie stretched.

"You should come out with me."

"To where?" Marnie knew the gossip around the hospital about Bianca flirting with a married doctor. She liked Bianca but didn't want to be involved in any drama that could mess up her chances of being promoted to supervisor.

"A lounge for drinks with me and a few girls."

It was nearing seven thirty when she pondered and checked her watch. She had two days off coming up and could use the time to catch up on sleep.

"One drink." Marnie held up a finger.

Bianca grinned and high-fived Marnie.

"I can conclude from the smiles on your faces that you've checked on all your patients." Charlotte Lopez was older than most of the nurses on staff. She ran the place like a well-oiled machine, and most of the doctors were scared of her and didn't want to ruffle any feathers. Her family was one of the highest donors, keeping the building up and running.

Bianca and Marnie put on a fake smile.

"Yes, we have, Mrs. Lopez," both answered at the same time.

Charlotte stared at both women, drew her nose up, and walked off. Marnie and Bianca burst into light giggles at the way Charlotte was about to argue them down if they were behind on work.

"I can't believe she's our boss," Bianca fussed.

Marnie stood and grabbed her jacket.

"Hopefully, she retires soon. I heard her position would be open."

"Are you thinking of applying?"

Marnie nodded and picked up her purse.

"Text me when you make it to the lounge," Bianca called out.

Marnie waved a hand and headed to the employee locker room to pick up her backpack.

* * *

TWO HOURS LATER.

"Bianca, how much longer are we going to stay out here?" her friend Tasha grumbled, shifting from one foot to the other.

Bianca looked down at her and typed in the message thread she had with Marnie.

Bianca: Hey, where are you?

Marnie: Forty minutes away.

Bianca: Marnie! Marnie!

The response never came, and Bianca was annoyed that they'd been outside waiting for over twenty minutes. Marnie texted thirty minutes ago and said she'd be there soon. They'd already gone in and came back out to see if she needed directions. Bianca liked Marnie and they'd become fast friends, but if she didn't want to hang out outside of work she should have told her beforehand.

"Your girl isn't coming."

"She's probably stuck in traffic."

Tasha threw her hands up in the air.

"Traffic, my ass."

"Let me text her again."

Tasha blew out a frustrated breath, snatched Bianca's phone out of her hand, and marched inside the lounge with her screaming behind her.

"Tasha! Give me my phone."

They made it to the booth they'd rented, and Tasha plopped down, passing her phone back.

"I'm done waiting. She either comes, or she doesn't." Tasha shrugged, motioning for the waitress to approach.

"Remind me to never worry about you."

"I won't. Besides, she probably got caught up with a guy."

"No, she was coming. Look at my messages." Bianca held her phone up.

Tasha pushed it away, snapping her fingers to the beat.

"Hi, ladies, what can I get you?" The waitress stood on the side of the women.

"Another mojito please and a small serve tacos."

Starlight was a two-story building that opened five years ago and became the go-to place for people to get to know each other, plus have dates. The lounge had everything from the dance floor, hookah setup, and stripper poles on the next level. A lot of people frowned upon strip lounges as a date location, but the owner made it work. Bianca came at least once a week to hang out.

"And for you, beautiful?"

"I'll have the same thing, and water please."

"Water!" Tasha choked on her drink.

"I'm driving, remember?"

"Girl! Tonight is about letting our hair loose." Tasha was single with no kids, and she didn't work besides dating old men with money to pay her bills.

"Unlike you, Tasha, I have responsibilities," Bianca reminded her best friend.

"Whatever."

"Coming right up." The waitress took the empty glasses off the table and headed back to the bar.

Bianca raised her phone to her ear and dialed Marnie's number one more time.

"You've reached Marnie. I can't come to the phone right now—" Bianca disconnected the call and sighed.

Their drinks arrived back at the table.

"Relax, your friend ditched you for some man. It's not the end of the world." Tasha lifted her mojito and clinked glasses with Bianca as the DJ changed the beat of the music to reggae tunes.

"You're right, and the bitch better have gotten a nice orgasm out of standing me up." Bianca slapped hands with Tasha as they laughed.

"That's what I'm talking about."

CHAPTER 2

Knock! Knock!

"Come in!"

When Jessica pushed the door open, she held up two coffee cups as Leo motioned for her to take a seat. While he spoke, she removed her bag off her shoulder, placed it on the floor, and sipped her coffee.

"No, I want the forensic team to send the report to me now." Leo reached over the desk and grabbed the hot coffee with light cream and two sugars.

"All right, thanks, John." Leo ended the call, took another sip of his coffee and then closed his eyes.

"Tough case?"

Leo sat up in his chair and faced Jessica.

"What are you doing here?" He moved the case file he'd just received last night off his desk into the awaiting document tray.

"I'm back in town."

"How was Townsend?"

"Good, it helped refresh me."

"Your parents?"

"Good. Stop changing the subject."

"Not changing the subject."

"Yes, you are."

"Shouldn't you be at the newspaper?"

"I'm going once I leave here."

"I don't have anything for you."

"Leoooo…" she whined.

"Serious, Jessica. Nothing is going on."

"The call you just took?"

"Nothing major, just a robbery."

"Fine, I'll leave you alone." Jessica stood right when the door opened.

"Detective Walsh?" Officer Young held a note in his hand.

"What's up, Kian?"

Kian passed the note to Leo.

"A body at Starlight Lounge," Officer Young replied.

Leo glanced at Jessica, and she looked off to avoid his glare.

"Thanks. Tell them to keep it locked down until I get there." Leo rose out of his seat.

Jessica started to walk out of his office.

"Where are you going?" Leo questioned and slid his arm in his jacket.

"To work."

"At the newspaper?" Leo stared in her eyes, and Jessica knew he could tell when she was lying, so she rushed out of his office.

"Jessica! Jessica!" Leo yelled as she jogged out of the police station. Everybody knew Jessica and how she operated. They didn't waste time to stop her because more than likely, she would be right back causing more trouble.

"Did I say something wrong?" Officer Young stood next

to Leo with a perplexed look on his face. Leo rubbed a hand down his face.

"No, just Jessica Smith and murder are not a great combination."

* * *

An hour later, Leo arrived on the scene, parked his car, and stepped out to a crowd of police and members of the media surrounding the Starlight building. He'd asked to have the place on lockdown, but the owner was already giving an interview to the media. He shook his head and stalked over to the alley of the building and walked under the yellow tape.

"What do you have?" Leo glanced at the body of a young woman without any clothes on except for her underwear, and her eyes were open.

"The employees found her early this morning, but the time of death was around nine. Once I get her back, I can be sure."

"Same as the Connor case," Leo muttered, rubbing his jaw.

"I noticed that as well," the medical examiner said.

"Shit!"

"I can't rule that out, but I won't put it out in the media just yet."

"Yeah, we don't need to worry anybody."

The body was placed in a body bag, and Leo glanced around the alley and noticed a trash bin in the corner. Lifting the top, nothing stood out, but he'd have his men take everything to be looked over.

"Noooo!"

When he heard a loud scream, Leo let the top go and

ran toward a familiar voice. He slid the gloves off and came around the corner to an officer holding Jessica back.

"Jessica." Leo jogged over to her, nodding for him to release her.

"She saw the body," the officer explained, and Leo glared at him.

"What does securing the evidence mean!" he snapped.

"Leo! He's back," Jessica cried in his chest.

"No, he's not, Jessica."

"That's Marnie." She sobbed in his arms.

"Who?"

"Marnie, my best friend."

"Shit!" He rubbed her back, walking her off to his car.

"Jessica! Jessica! Do you have a comment about the body that was discovered?" A reporter pointed a microphone in her face.

"No comment! Get them out of here," Leo barked, shoving his way through the crowd. He opened the door of his car and helped Jessica to sit. He dropped to his knees and gripped her hands.

"Leo, I... I... he killed my best friend." Jessica burst into tears.

"Let me get you home."

"No! I'm not leaving until I get some answers."

"Jessica."

"You can't protect me from this." Jessica wiped the tears from her face.

Leo cursed under his breath, removed his keys from his pocket, and stood.

"Where's your car?"

Jessica pointed down the street. Often she'd walk a block or two to keep her car hidden because everyone knew what she drove.

"Give me your keys."

"Why?"

"I'll drive you home and have someone take your car."

Jessica removed her keys and passed them over. All her thoughts jumbled in confusion. No matter how hard she tried, the past would continue to make its way back into her life. Leo shut the door and went to talk to another officer, pointing at Jessica's car to bring it to her apartment.

"Tell me about your friend." Leo made a turn at the light and headed on the freeway.

They were about twenty minutes away from downtown and her apartment building in the city.

"Marnie's a nurse. My best friend next to Allison and Lainey; we all grew up together"

"When's the last time you talked to her?"

"Maybe a month ago."

"Why so long?"

"She travels as a nurse sometimes for extra money."

"Do you know anyone who would hurt her?"

"No."

"I'm sorry, Jess."

"It's all my fault."

"Hey, don't think like that." He covered her palm.

"Leo, I'm cursed."

"The world is fucked up, but this is not your fault. We'll catch whoever did this to your friend."

"I know he's dead, but… the way she was—"

Leo grasped her hand.

"He can't hurt you, and I promise we'll catch the person who did this to Marnie."

When Leo arrived at her apartment and turned the car off, he jumped out and walked around to help her out.

"You don't have to walk me up."

"Jessica."

"No, I need to be alone." Her world was falling down

around her again as Jessica walked away and headed inside her building in tears. When she saw her neighbor, she waved and took the elevator up to her floor. Closing her apartment door behind her, she dropped her bag on the table, took off her jacket, and started toward the fridge for a bottle of water. She walked into her office and opened the door. Taking a moment to gaze at her wall of plaques, she turned on the light. As she sat at her desk, she opened her file cabinet and retrieved everything related to the murders that Connor committed in her hometown. She promised Leo that Marnie wouldn't languish like other unsolved cases if she did her own side investigations. However, Leo was unaware Jessica had been doing so. It was hard to look at the photos of her close friends, but she pushed through and read about how the bodies laid, checking if they matched up to Marnie.

"Talk to me, Marnie," Jessica muttered.

Jessica tapped her pen on the desk, logged into her computer, and looked up any murders for the few days before Marnie and after. Pausing at the photos of the barn in Tennessee where it all started, Jessica turned slowly, picked up her phone, and dialed Lainey's number. It was late in Tennessee, but she needed to hear her voice.

"Jess, what's wrong?" Lainey groggily answered.

Jessica wiped a tear from her cheek.

"I needed to hear your voice."

"You all right?"

Her voice felt shaky.

"Not really. I have to tell you something."

"What is it, Jessica?"

"Marnie was killed."

"Oh. My, God." Jessica heard movement in the background.

"Lainey, I'm sorry."

"I could come out there for a little bit."

"No, you don't have to do that. You have kids and a husband."

"What time is it there?"

"Late, I need to get to bed." Jessica mulled over how she would navigate with Leo not leaving her out of the discussion.

"Marnie and Allison would want us to keep their names alive."

"You're right." Jessica stood, twisted the knob on the door, walked to the bathroom, and looked at herself in the mirror, noticing the bags forming.

"I won't hold you any longer. I'll call you soon."

"All right, Jess. Don't disappear on me."

"I promise." Jessica pulled the phone from her ear and held it under her chin for a second, thinking.

CHAPTER 3

Two days later, Bianca sat at her desk at the hospital and scanned over the monitors of patients. She still hadn't heard from Marnie but figured she'd stroll in today with a smile on her face after ditching them for a guy.

"I need you to stay longer today," Charlotte expressed.

"I can't."

"You've been late twice last month, and I let you slide," Charlotte demanded, staring at Bianca.

"That's not fair, Charlotte."

Charlotte held her hand up.

"Mrs. Lopez." Bianca rubbed her temples. She tried to stay polite and respect her elders, since the woman was in her late fifties and had worked at the hospital for many years.

"Excuse me." Jessica cleared her voice.

Charlotte stood straight with her back to the nurses' desk. Bianca peered at the young woman.

"Yes, can I help you?" Charlotte spoke.

"I'm looking for Charlotte Lopez."

"That's me. How can I help you?"

"I'm Jessica. A friend of Marnie's."

Charlotte's nose turned up in disgust. That was the reason she needed Bianca to stay late; Marnie was out doing God knows what and not attending to her duties.

"Well, if you're a friend of Marnie's, please relay the message that she's fired."

Bianca gasped in shock.

"Marnie's dead," Jessica responded, and both women froze in shock.

"Dead!" Bianca jumped out of her chair.

"Bianca, please keep your voice down," Charlotte reprimanded.

"Marnie's my best friend, and I wanted to clean out her things."

"How did she die?" Bianca questioned.

Jessica didn't think it was her place to spill the exact details, but she felt it was only right to let them know as women.

"She was murdered."

"What! I just spoke to her two days ago," Bianca explained, and Jessica's eyes rose in surprise.

"Where?"

"We were meeting up at Starlight," Bianca confessed, and Jessica reached in her pocket and grabbed her phone to call Leo.

"What time? I need you to speak with the police."

Charlotte looked from Jessica to Bianca and didn't want a flurry of police in the hospital to cause further disturbance.

"Sorry about your friend, but I can't have my employee leave right now or have police up here."

"It'll only take a minute," Jessica pleaded as the phone dialed.

"I understand, but Marnie was supposed to work today, and she called out."

Jessica's nostrils flared, glancing at the name badge on her shirt.

"My best friend is dead." Jessica ended the call.

"Bianca can speak with the police on her off time. Sorry, we have a hospital to run."

Charlotte walked off and left Jessica with her mouth hanging open in shock.

"Ignore her."

"Is she always like that?" Jessica wondered.

"Unfortunately, yes."

"I can walk you to the employee lockers, I doubt Marnie left anything."

Bianca escorted Jessica toward the back entrance and pushed the button to open the door to the employee area. The breakroom had lockers lined up against the wall. Around the corner held beds for when people worked the graveyard shifts.

"Here's her locker." Bianca pointed. Jessica held Marnie's keys and unlocked the locker just to find it empty.

"Empty."

"She usually keeps a jacket, purse, and maybe books." Bianca headed to the fridge to grab a bottle of water and took a seat at the table.

"Tell me about the night you went to Starlight." Jessica removed her pen and notebook to take notes.

"We both worked that night and got off at eight. She left before me."

"What type of mood was she in?"

"Fine to me. We planned to meet up, and I told her to text me when she made it to the lounge."

"What time was that?"

"I'm not sure because she never came."

"Huh…" Jessica paused when she answered.

"She never made it into the lounge."

"Wait, did she call and say she would be late?"

"No, just texted to say she was forty minutes away."

"Do you still have the messages?"

Bianca nodded and reached in her pocket to grab her phone. She scrolled to the thread and handed the phone to Jessica.

"Nothing after you texted Marnie?" Jessica mumbled.

"I tried to dial her number, but a voice message came up."

"She was found outside the club in the alley."

Bianca held a hand up to her mouth in shock as tears fell down her cheeks.

"I could have helped her." Bianca held her face in her hands and cried.

"Whoever did this will be caught. I promise."

Bianca wiped her face.

"Marnie was nice to me."

"Marnie and I grew up together in Tennessee."

"Really?"

"Well, during the summer, I'd visit my grandparents, and she lived there. Along with my other friends…" Jessica's voice drifted off.

"Marnie's lucky to have you," Bianca commented, and Jessica's lip curved into a smile.

"Can I have your phone number in case I have more questions?"

"What work do you do? I forgot to ask when you dialed the police. Are you a detective?"

"A reporter for the newspaper."

"Wow."

"Not that fabulous of a job; it couldn't save my friends."

"Friends?"

Jessica didn't know how conversations would go with people when they found out two of her best friends were killed. As time went on, she thought she was cursed.

"Uhm, you know the killing of the young women with only their underwear on?"

"Yeah, I saw it on the news."

"One of them was my other best friend Allison."

"Was Marnie killed like that?" Bianca hesitated.

Jessica nodded, and Bianca rose out of her seat.

"Oh my God! What if they saw my number when I called?" Bianca panicked.

"Bianca, calm down." Jessica tried to rub her back, but Bianca stiffened.

"Please leave me alone."

"Sorry."

The door opened, and Charlotte glared at both women.

"Bianca, who told you to leave the nurses' station?" Charlotte argued.

"It's my fault. Please don't blame her." Jessica tried to diffuse the situation.

"You're not allowed back here. Either you leave quietly, or I'll call the police," Charlotte complained.

"Bianca, please call me if you think of anything." Jessica passed her card toward Bianca.

* * *

THIRTY MINUTES LATER, Jessica arrived at the Starlight Lounge. It had opened back up after being shut down while they worked on the case. Leo told her to stay away, but she couldn't sleep at night without finding out Marnie's last moments. The bouncer let her through, and she glanced around at the crowd of people talking and drinking like nothing ever happened a few nights ago.

"You look lost," the bartender yelled, and Jessica sat on the stool and removed her ID from her purse.

"What did you hear the night of the killing?"

He looked down at her badge and started to walk off. Jessica grasped his hand.

"Wait! Please. I just have a few questions."

"I don't talk to reporters."

"Please, the girl who was killed is my best friend."

"Sorry, but I can't help you."

Jessica looked at the bar, then sat back on the stool.

"Can I get a rum and Coke?"

"Rum and Coke. Sure."

He wiped the counter down and placed a coaster in front of her.

The bartender was about five nine in height with light-brown skin and his hair pulled back in a ponytail.

"How long have you worked here?" Jessica knew her reporter skills would need to kick in to soften him up.

"About three years."

"Is it always this busy?"

He placed the drink down.

"Thanks." Jessica saluted him and took a sip.

"Almost every night is crowded."

"Except the past two days, right?" Jessica watched as his jawline twitched and his hands turned to fists.

"Look, I could get in a lot of trouble if I talk to you."

"I understand. A few questions, and then I'm gone."

"I worked the night she was killed."

"Did you see anything or anyone that stood out?"

"No, it was a typical night, and the music was loud, so I doubt we heard a scream."

"How often do fights happen here?"

"Not very much."

"Do you have cameras here?"

"Yeah, but I doubt if the owner will let you watch them."

"Is he here tonight?"

"No, he's off."

Jessica continued to sip on her drink slowly.

"Who takes the trash out at night typically?"

"Either me or the waitstaff." He walked over to a couple and took their orders. Jessica took out her phone and texted Leo.

Jessica: We need to meet.

Leo: I'm at the station.

Jessica: Can you come to my place?

Leo: Is this an emergency?

"Any other questions?" He stood in front of her.

"No, that's all. Thanks."

Jessica removed money from her wallet and paid her tab.

Jessica: No.

Leo: I'll call you tomorrow.

Jessica blew out a breath, closed her messages, and stood up from the chair.

"If you think of anything else, please call me." Jessica wrote her cell phone number on the back of the card.

"Jessica Smith." He read the name aloud and watched her stroll out of the lounge. She stared out in the parking structure, remembering the alley was the place where Marnie was found dead. Jessica removed her phone, turned on the flashlight, and scanned the ground and up the wall to the top of the building to see if any cameras were working in the area. A chill ran up her spine at the coldness and loneliness she must have felt at knowing this was her last moment.

"Aye. What are you doing back there?" An older homeless man dropped the bag of cans in his hand near the dumpster.

"Are you out here often?"

Jessica held the phone down.

He waved her off.

Jessica reached in her pocket and pulled out some money.

"Here, please tell me anything if you know something."

"I don't know anything, lady," he mumbled, lifting the trash lid and sifting through for bottles.

"What about another twenty?"

She started to pass him more money when he snatched it out of her hand and slipped it in his pocket.

"I don't know anything. All I heard were screams," he muttered, drunkenly stumbling off.

As she watched him stammer away, she shook her head and moved further in the alley to the dead end and saw a few words scribbled on the wall that spelled out *one*. She couldn't tell if that had anything to do with the death of her friend, but she took a snapshot as some type of evidence. Jessica inhaled deeply, steadied herself, and walked from the alleyway to her car.

CHAPTER 4

A week later.

He'd gotten a chance to feed his appetite with the first girl at Starlight Lounge. It was a trial run, and he didn't want any mistakes to come up now that he'd been following the news reports. Every night, he studied what Connor accomplished, and he admired his techniques. Often, the news would label what he did as wrong, or call him crazy, but he felt the opposite. In his mind, it was the right thing to do. The women nowadays weren't clean, and most times, they tried to emasculate him. The abuse he grew up around and the abandonment by his mother ultimately made his decision to seek comfort in hurting women as a stamp of righting the wrongs he endured. The power he felt between his hands showed he was in charge, and no one could stop the goal of death and cleansing the world of women who turned away from him. The activity in front of him jarred him from his thoughts.

"What did you say?"

"I said it's going to be ten dollars and twenty cents," the older woman spoke and placed the bag on the counter.

"Thanks." He removed his wallet from his pocket and slid his card in the machine.

"Here's your receipt." She pushed the bag of paint in front of him.

"Thanks again."

It wasn't too cold on a Sunday afternoon, so he decided to work on his side project in the backyard of his home. The shed was close to being finished after he added in new wood panels, baseboards, and shelves. The paint he picked up would bring it more to life with the off-eggshell color. All of his tools laid on the floor, perfectly wrapped in plastic and ready to be organized after the paint dried.

Returning to his car, he shut the car door and slid the belt over his waist. He smiled at the blonde woman in blue shorts and tank top walking toward the door of the outlet store. He started to open the door and get out to greet her when he noticed a gentleman run up behind her and wrap his arms around her waist.

"Bitch," he mumbled, leaving the lot.

Those types of men were gullible in his mind. They were stupid for falling for her type. All they did was use men until their pockets were dry. Then they dump you for the next rich man that came along. Honestly, he felt pity for all men who didn't know how to control their women.

"Dummies." He chuckled, turned the radio up, and drove home.

A few minutes later, he arrived home, parked in the driveway, and waved at his neighbor as he closed the door. The old lady was annoying; she kept gossiping about everyone in the area and tried to set him up on a blind date with her daughter who stood him up. The older woman apologized and tried to hook him up with her niece. He declined because she was a police officer, and he'd prefer to not have eyes judging him constantly. He removed the jacket, carried the bag outside, unlocked the shed door, stepped inside to his sanctuary, and dropped the bag of paint on the bench. He stood back, crossed his arms over his chest, and stared at the pictures of potential women he'd studied for the last few days.

"Too many to choose from," he muttered, removed the paint, and turned on his Beethoven. After two hours of painting, he nodded to the music, added the empty containers to the trash bag, and walked out to the front of the house to place it in the trash bin.

"Cleaning again?" Anna turned the water hose off in her yard and strolled toward him. Her five-foot-two height and white hair hung low in a ponytail, she stared and smiled.

He smiled, lifted the lid, and tossed both bags inside.

"Never can be too clean."

"You know, my niece asked me about you."

He wiped the sweat off his forehead.

"I told you, Anna, I'm too busy to date." He looked down at his watch.

Anna couldn't understand why a handsome young man would turn down so many dates. She rarely saw women come over to his place at night, or family and friends.

"You need a good woman in your life."

He cocked his head to the side and looked at her.

"Good woman."

Anna shook her head in answer.

"Most guys your age go out, party, and drink."

"I'm not like most guys." He shifted and headed back to the shed. Anna watched him walk away.

"Must be a virgin," Anna muttered.

* * *

AFTER WORK THE NEXT NIGHT, he drove down to the riverfront section that housed a movie theater, club, bowling alley, and restaurants. It was the best place to find a new person to intrigue his appetite since the last kill. He stepped out of the car and slid his jacket on, checking his hair in the side mirror before strolling to the front door of the bar. After showing his ID, he walked through the front crowd of couples standing at the bar and making out. He glared and shifted to the end of the bar near the bartender to order.

"What are you drinking?"

"Vodka and Sprite."

"Coming up."

His head turned at the loud laughter coming from the corner. His left eye twitched as he opened and closed his fist. He turned his head back to the bar and sipped his drink. He closed his eyes and visualized how he would trace his hand along her throat and down her chest with his knife. Time was ticking as his urges spoke in his head to take her home. After gulping the rest of his drink down, he raised his hand and motioned for the bartender to bring another one.

"Oops, sorry," a sweet, sultry voice said, treading toward the bartender.

"No problem," he replied, staring as she talked to the bartender. Two hours later, she walked out of the bar with her friend, hugged her, then climbed in her car and pulled out of the parking structure. He followed as she drove down the street. Five minutes went by when she turned on her signal to pull over on the dark road as the tire went out.

Knock!

She rolled down the window.

"Everything okay?" he questioned.

She blew out a breath.

"I think I have a flat tire. Do you mind if I use your phone? Mine died." She held her head against the steering wheel.

"My boys took my phone by accident, I can drive you to the closest gas station, and you can call a tow truck," he lied, and she allowed any thoughts of him being dangerous out of the window when he started to walk off.

"Wait! Let me grab my purse."

He smiled, walked back over to her car, and opened the door to help her grab everything.

"You look familiar."

"We bumped into each other at the bar earlier."

"Oh right. Thanks for helping me."

He opened the passenger door for her to climb in and shut it before jogging around to the driver's door.

"No problem. Can't have a pretty girl like you out here for any weirdo to pick up." He grinned, pulled on the road, and drove off.

CHAPTER 5

essica sat on top of Leo's desk and waited for him to come back in from the kitchen. All night, she tossed and turned after a long night of working on a new story for the paper. Her boss gave her a little leeway to mourn her friend's death, but she seemed to be more focused on finding the killer, instead of doing her job. Leo opened the door, pointed to the chair in front of his desk for her to sit, and held a cup of coffee out for her to take. Leo stayed silent and stared at Jessica. Her left brow rose in curiosity.

"I didn't do what you were thinking." Jessica sipped on her coffee.

Leo placed his coffee down, sighed, and opened the file folder on his desk.

"Why do I have information about you looking into Marnie's case?"

Jessica looked away, clenching her teeth.

"Jessica, we've talked about this before."

"Leo, how do you think I feel about both of my best friends being killed?"

He stood up and walked around the desk to sit on the edge, grabbing her hands.

"I can't imagine what you're going through, but this is putting you in danger if you pursue this case. Let the police handle everything." Little did Leo know that Jessica would fight tooth and nail to get the killer found.

"Can you tell me any updates?"

Leo grunted, stood, and headed back to his chair.

"No camera footage; it was too dark."

"What about the homeless guy I talked to? Maybe he can remember something."

"It's a dead end, Jess."

Jessica twisted the cup in front of her.

Knock! Knock!

"Yeah!"

"I got a call that another girl was found." Judy, an older officer, has been with the department for twenty years.

"Thanks, Judy." Leo groaned, picked up the phone, and called the chief.

"Where was the body found?"

Judy glanced from Jessica to Leo in nervousness at her question.

"Jess," Leo muttered.

"Sorry."

Judy walked out of the room.

"Yes, Chief. Heading out now." Leo wrote something down on a piece of paper and hung up. He pulled the sheet of paper off the notepad, stood, and grabbed his jacket.

"I'm going with you."

"No, you're not." Leo adjusted his jacket.

"Either I ride with you, or I can follow you in my car." Jessica planted her hand on her hip.

He gripped his keys, opened the door, and motioned for her to walk ahead. Leo shut the door and walked down the hall as Jessica rambled on that she wouldn't interrupt his investigation.

"Leo!"

Both of them turned at the sound of his name being called.

"You get the information for me?"

"Right here. Where are you headed?" Kian held out the file box.

"A crime scene. Can you leave it on my desk, and I'll check it out later?"

"For sure. What's up, Jessica?" He lifted the box and turned toward the direction of Leo's office.

"Hey, Kian. What's in the box?"

"Boring stuff." Kian joked, walking backwards.

"Don't remind me." Leo put his shades on, then strolled out of the building to his car.

"When we get there, you remember to leave the questions to me."

"Yes, sir." Jessica sat back and placed her seat belt on.

* * *

LEO PUSHED at the side of the door until it popped open and walked through the apartment as the police directed people to keep a safe distance. He could feel the pressure mount to stop the killer before he struck again, or the chief would pull him off the case. Jessica bumped into his back when he stopped suddenly.

"Sorry."

"Don't move," Leo said.

"I won't."

"Hey, Leo, she's back here." Another officer on the scene directed him with a wave.

Jessica scanned the living room, and it looked like a

typical single woman's apartment, with a gray couch by a fireplace, wide windows overlooking a deck, and a book-shelf—all the things she had at home. After she watched Leo leave, she peered over to the table and noticed a book open and glanced over her shoulder to see if anyone was watching. She slid her gloves on, stalked over and leaned down to turn it over. It was a Stephen King novel. As she glossed through the pages, she noticed a remote, keys, and shoes on the floor.

"Did you remove them or the killer," Jessica mumbled to herself.

"All right, bag her up and send me the report," Leo ordered, and Jessica clamored to get back to her original spot.

Leo sharply stopped, and his brows dipped at Jessica as she fidgeted with her hands.

"What did you find?" Jessica inquired.

"Another victim." Leo removed his phone from his pocket and checked the time.

"Same as Marnie?"

"Do you have to be at the newspaper?"

"Unfortunately, I do. Why?"

"I'll drop you off after we grab something to eat."

"What about my car?"

"I'll have one of the patrolmen bring it up there." He held out his hand for her keys.

Jessica slipped them in his hands.

"Make sure you drop off her vehicle. It's parked in the visitor section with a press tag on the front." Leo passed the keys to the patrolman and guided Jessica out of the room. Thirty minutes later, they arrived at the cafe a few blocks from her job.

"Hello, you two," Gilda, the longtime waitress at the café, spoke.

"Gilda, what are the specials today?" Leo asked.

"Same as always, tuna melt or omelet and French toast," Gilda kidded.

"Sign me up for the French toast," Leo answered.

"What about you, Jessica?" Gilda questioned.

"Omelet please."

"Coming right up. Drinks will be out in a second." Gilda shifted and headed to submit their order. Jessica laid her hands on the top of the table and stared at Leo.

"What?" Leo asked.

"Tell me what you found, Leo."

"Jessica, this is police business."

"I know that, and I've been doing my own research," Jessica whispered.

"How and with whom?" His brows crinkled.

"Nobody but me." She pointed at herself.

"You've got to be kidding me." He ran a hand down his face. She began to reply when Gilda approached the table with their food. Leo cut into the French toast.

Leo leaned back in his seat and resisted the urge to tell Jessica this was a bad idea to go on a hunt for a serial killer they had no idea about. The door opened, and a few young women walked in laughing together.

"Did you forget what happened last time?" Leo muttered in frustration.

"That's the reason you should let me help."

Leo folded his hands.

Clearly, Jessica wouldn't listen to anything Leo said about searching on her own.

Leo picked up his drink and took a gulp.

"I don't want a repeat of last time. I'll think about what I would share."

"All I ask, Leo."

"Food is on me." Leo dropped his napkin on the table,

and they continued to eat as they discussed what he found at the apartment.

Two bodies staged in the same way with the same cuts in only underwear put Leo on high alert. He'd have to figure out if a serial killer was on the loose or a copycat of Connor.

CHAPTER 6

*B*ianca approached the receptionist desk at the newspaper, and they pointed her in the direction of the elevator and two doors down on the third floor. Bianca had little sleep since Marnie's murder, and she wanted to find out after another death was reported on the news, if Jessica had any insight. Bianca lightly tapped on the door.

"Open," Jessica yelled.

Bianca turned the knob and smiled at Jessica.

"Bianca, right?" Jessica placed the phone down on the receiver.

"Sorry to come to your job, but I was hesitant to talk to the police."

"You're fine. Have a seat."

Bianca removed her purse and placed it on her lap.

"How are you doing?"

"Not the best. Work has kept me busy."

"I've been in that position before."

Jessica inhaled the remnants of her smoothie.

"Have you heard anything about who hurt Marnie?"

"No, but Leo is going to keep me updated."

"Who's Leo?"

"A cop that I know."

"Do you trust him?"

"With my life."

"Work has been weird since her death."

Jessica flicked an eyebrow up and down in acknowledgement.

"I found myself calling her number in the middle of the night one day, then I remembered. We'd just started our friendship, and she was sweet and kind." Her voice choked.

Jessica reached a hand over and covered her palm.

"Bianca, I can't imagine what it was like that night, but Marnie would want you to move forward."

Bianca wiped a tear from her cheek

"I know this might seem crazy, but I have very few friends, and you seem cool. Marnie talked about her friend group."

Jessica rose from her seat and came around to hug Bianca.

"We can hang out anytime."

"Thanks, I need to get to work, and I won't keep you any longer." Bianca got to her feet.

Jessica grabbed her cell and checked her calendar.

"How about dinner tomorrow night?"

"I'd love that."

"Great! Come to my place. We'll have wine and a full meal." They exchanged numbers.

"Should I bring anything?"

"Yourself." Jessica grinned, hugging her again.

Bianca walked out of her office. Jessica held the door, and her boss approached.

"Jessica, we need to talk."

"Sure, what's up?" Jessica leaned against her door.

"Are you done with the Texas oil story?"

Jessica shook her head.

Her editor took a minute.

"Do you want to be here, Jessica?"

"What kind of question is that?"

"Your lack of research in stories, never on time… Shall I go on?"

Jessica moved toward her desk. She relaxed into her seat, groaned and rubbed her forehead.

"This isn't personal, Jessica."

"Seems like all you do is dig into me."

"I need the story on my desk by the end of the week," he demanded and walked away from her door.

* * *

JESSICA HEADED down the aisle of the grocery store and picked up a bag of chicken, rice, and vegetables. She'd spent the entire day catching up on work that she'd put off while she looked into what happened to Marnie. She arrived at the wine aisle and stared between the red and white bottles.

"With chicken, I hear white works best." Kian chuckled, holding a basket in his hand with flowers.

"Hey, Kian. What are you doing here?"

Kian held up a basket.

"Bachelor life." He laughed.

"Bachelorette life." Jessica pointed at the wine and chuckled.

"Do you live around here?"

"I do. The office is up the block, and my place is a few blocks from there."

"Cool. We didn't see you at the station today." Kian glanced at her.

Jessica grabbed two bottles of wine and placed them in her cart.

"Leo is probably happy I didn't show up." Jessica caught Kian's stare and shoved her cart forward. Kian walked alongside her to the front of the store.

"Probably true." Kian stood behind Jessica.

Jessica pulled her items from the cart toward the cashier. Kian grabbed his phone from his pocket and texted.

Jessica passed her credit card to pay.

"Let me get that for you."

"You don't have to do that, Kian."

"My pleasure." Kian bumped her shoulder.

"Thanks. I owe you," Jessica said and grabbed the two bags.

"How about you pay me back with dinner?" Kian took his things from the basket and slid the card in to pay.

Jessica slid a strand of hair from her face.

"How old are you, Kian?"

"Twenty-five."

"Young."

"Young but mature."

Kian escorted Jessica to her car.

"Well, Kian, thanks for everything, but I'll have to pass on dinner."

Kian nodded in understanding.

"No worries. I won't hold it against you." Kian chortled and strolled to his car across from Jessica in the parking lot. She slid the key in the ignition, pulled on her seat belt, and headed home. An hour later, she'd put her groceries away and turned on the TV to the latest favorite show she'd recorded. She dimmed the lights, curled up on the couch, then cut into her baked potato and spaghetti. Slipping a blanket over her legs and grinning at the comedian, someone knocked on her door. Jessica paused the TV, put her plate on the table, and stood to open the door.

"Hey, Adam."

"The police and fire department are here."

"Really? Why?"

"I guess someone broke into the building and trashed one of the apartments."

"Seriously!" Jessica crossed her arms, looked out the door, and saw the building manager and policeman talking.

"Are you missing anything?"

"No, I mean I haven't really looked."

"Just be careful."

"Thanks, Adam." Jessica closed the door and reached over to lift the remote and turned the show back on. She grabbed her laptop to work on the story she needed to turn into her editor.

Ring!

"Hello."

"Hey, Jessica. It's Bianca."

"Is something wrong, Bianca?"

"I'm not sure."

Jessica sat up straight at the concern in her voice.

"Well, I was coming home, and I felt like someone was following me."

"Did you see anyone?"

"No, and I feel foolish if I'm being honest."

"You're not foolish. Tell me exactly what happened."

"It felt like a different chill in the air. I looked behind me, but no one was there."

"With everything going on, I can understand."

"Do you think I should call the police? I don't want to be another victim."

"Something to be aware of for sure. I can talk to Leo and maybe assign someone to watch your place."

"Thanks, Jessica."

"Leo is someone I trust, we can talk with him together."

"That would be nice."

"Okay, I'll be able to meet you soon."

Bang!

"Oh, shit!" Jessica dropped her phone.

"Jessica! Is everything okay?" She picked her phone up.

The fire alarm went off in the building

"Bianca, I need to call you back."

"Are you all right?"

"Not sure, but there might be a fire in my building."

"That's terrible. Call me if you need anything."

Jessica hurriedly hung up and dialed Leo's number.

All of the lights in the building went out.

"Shit."

"Hello."

"Leo! Leo! It's Jessica," she whispered.

"Why are you whispering?"

"I heard a loud blast, and then the lights went out."

"Don't leave your apartment. I'll send some guys to you."

"That's the thing… some police and firemen are here already."

"What do you mean?"

"I guess we had someone break in earlier today."

"Keep me on the line."

Jessica slid the curtain back in her window and noticed an ambulance and fire truck outside.

"It's him."

"Who?"

"Connor."

"Jessica, he's gone."

"Just hurry up, Leo."

"On my way."

CHAPTER 7

The next day, Leo poured coffee in his cup and rubbed his eyes from not sleeping at all. He frowned at the empty container of milk, tossed it in the trash, and grabbed another cup for Jessica. After he arrived last night, he spoke with the police in charge and found out some kids were playing in the building and set off the alarm. Leo passed the coffee to Jessica. She thanked him and raised her legs up on top of the couch.

"I appreciate you staying last night."

"Did you sleep at all?"

"No," she huffed.

"At least it was just some kids."

"Only reason I feel like I can breathe better."

"Are you hungry?"

"No, I need to get to work." Jessica stretched and rose from the couch.

"I'm heading to the station. Call me if anything else happens." Leo put his cup on the table and strolled to the door.

"Call me later."

"Relax, Jessica, you stress too much." Leo clapped her on the shoulder.

"Be careful today." Jessica shut the door behind him, leaned against it, and sighed. Leo's comment sat in the back of her mind. Once she was dressed, with her bag in her hand, she strolled to her car and climbed in to head to the hospital before work to check on Bianca. She started the car and headed in the direction of her favorite bakery shop to grab something to eat. Her Bluetooth rang, and she answered to speak with her mom.

"Hey, Mom."

"How are you, Jess?"

"One day at a time as usual."

"I spoke with Lainey."

Nervousness erupted in her stomach, as she slowed down at the red light.

"It was a bad night, and I needed to talk to my friend."

"This is really disturbing. Two of your friends, Jess."

Jessica sped up through traffic. A few minutes later she picked up her favorite bagel and coffee. Started back on her destination.

"Don't worry, Mom. Leo has been a big help."

"As a mother, I never stop worrying."

Jessica pulled into the parking lot of the hospital

"Mom, I just arrived at work. Can I call you later?"

"All right, sweetie. Don't forget."

Jessica grabbed her purse and stepped out of the car. The double doors opened, and Jessica went to the nurses' station.

"Hi, can you tell me if Bianca is working today?"

"She should be," a nurse answered and handed over a visitor badge.

"Thanks."

Jessica's head snapped up when she saw Kian come toward her through the door.

"Hey, Jess."

"Kian, what are you doing here?"

"Leo had me come with him to check on a contact."

"Is he here?" Jessica glanced around.

"No, he called out sick."

"I just saw him the other day, he looked fine."

"Maybe it's a twenty-four hour bug." Kian answered.

"Oh, I'll have to check up on him." Jessica started to walk off when Kian grasped her hand.

"I wanted to see how you're doing. I heard what happened."

"What do you mean?"

"The apartment last night." Kian's eyes bore into hers.

"Jessica, I didn't know you were here." Bianca approached and held her arm out for a hug.

"I need to get back to the station." Kian smiled and stalked away.

"Okay," Jessica replied with a small grin.

"Who was that?" Bianca breathed out.

"Kian, he's a police officer."

"Oh, he's cute."

Jessica giggled.

Bianca reclined in her seat at the nurses' station.

"I came to check in on you." Jessica leaned on the counter.

"Thanks, I'm fine now." Bianca shuffled the papers in front of her.

"If you still need to talk or anything, let me know."

"We need a doctor!" EMTs burst through the emergency doors with an unconscious woman on a stretcher. Bianca jumped up from the chair.

"What happened?"

"She was found in the park like this," he responded and continued to work on her.

"Jessica, I have to take care of this."

"I won't hold you. I hope she's all right."

"She was touch and go," the EMT said.

An alarm in her head went off.

* * *

Jessica charged through the police station hours later and demanded to speak with Leo about the incident at the hospital.

"Where is he?" Jessica tried to come around the door to the back.

"Out."

"Come on, Eric. I need to know what's going on with the copycat killer."

"We don't talk to reporters."

He blocked her with his hand.

"Don't you want to come from behind the desk and make a real change?" Jessica scanned his desk.

"Is this one of those times you try to manipulate me into letting you back there?"

"Fine, I'll call him on his cell phone," Jessica huffed, whirled around, and stomped off.

"You should stay in your lane, Jessica, and leave the police work for the professionals."

Jessica pushed the door open and paced back and forth in exasperation.

"Come on, Leo. Answer the phone."

"Jessica, you have bad timing as usual," Leo answered, loud music cutting him off.

Jessica attempted to call back, and the phone just rang.

"Leo! Leo!"

"Sorry, Jess, I'm out on a case. I can't talk."

"I need to meet with you now."

"Can't. I'm out in the Bronx on a case."

"What about tomorrow? There's been a break in the copycat killer."

"Jess, I told you to stay away from anything that has to do with Marnie's case."

"I would have, but a woman was brought into the hospital, and she survived."

"What makes you think it has anything to do with Marnie?"

"I have no reason to think it doesn't."

"We can talk about it tomorrow."

"Kian was there."

"Kian Young?"

"At the hospital."

"Yes, maybe you can see if he knows anything."

"Jess, he's still wet behind the ears. Leave it alone," Leo ordered and ended the conversation. She contemplated if she should go back to the station and demand that someone go up to the hospital, but she had another idea in mind, and no one could stop her from going. Jessica took off toward her car, threw her bag in the passenger seat, and headed for the park where the young woman was found. If she avoided any police that knew Leo, her plan could work. Then she'd have something to bring to the chief of police or maybe even higher, to the commissioner.

Jessica arrived minutes later and parked. She glanced around the park at a few couples and kids playing, but most was sectioned away with police tape. Jessica grabbed her cell phone and keys, shut the door, and strolled toward the roped-off area. She looked around to see if anyone noticed her and stepped in the bathroom. Fairly clean for an outdoors bathroom, she pushed each stall open.

"Show me what I'm missing," Jessica muttered to herself. She stalked over to the sink and bent down, but nothing stood out.

"What are you doing?"

Jessica was startled and jumped up, fidgeting with her keys and phone.

"Hi, I was just using the restroom."

In response, the officer narrowed his eyes.

"The sign out front said no entry."

"I didn't see the sign."

"The big yellow tape wasn't a clue?"

Jessica laughed.

"Sorry, I had to go really bad." He blocked her path as she went to walk around him.

"Who are you really?"

She sighed and took a step back.

"I work for the newspaper."

He snapped his finger.

"I knew it! You're late; the reporters already came."

"I see that. Were you here when it happened?" Jessica tried to pry.

"My lips are zipped. If anyone gets wind of me in the paper, I'll lose my job, lady."

"True, or you could become a hero."

"How?"

"Work with me to find the killer."

He scoffed.

"That'll for sure get me in trouble. Sorry, you have to leave."

"Okay." Jessica slipped out of the bathroom and released a breath.

Reluctantly, she needed to start from the beginning. Ronald stood guard outside the bathroom and put her farther away from finding the real killer. Jessica checked the time on her watch and remembered she promised to catch up with Lainey and her parents soon. As she lightly strolled to her car and checked her messages, her stomach growled. Then the phone vibrated.

"He can wait." She mumbled at seeing the name of her boss scrolled across.

CHAPTER 8

"All right! I need everyone to be quiet!" the captain blurted throughout the conference room.

"Captain! Why are we here so early?" a deputy inquired, leaning over to pick up a donut.

"Because we've had three women that fit the mold of Connor Little's work," he answered.

"Any updates on the young woman?" Kian questioned.

"Right now, she's unconscious. Once we get someone in to talk to her, we will be able to pinpoint some stuff."

"Captain, do we have a timeline of her incident?" Leo brought up, slipping sugar in his coffee cup.

"Not a lot to go on. She was attacked in the park."

"Probably random," another officer chimed in and shrugged.

"We can't take that chance. As of right now, I want extra men patrolling."

"Come on, Captain," everyone grumbled at the same time.

"Captain's right. Until we get a good idea on who's behind these killings, we can't slack off," Leo replied.

"The coroner stated the second victim was found in bed with only a bra and panties, no DNA." The captain motioned at the photos on the screen.

"Time of death?"

"Between eleven and one a.m.," the captain said.

"Can we assume it's the same person, or like Bobby said, it could be random?" Leo commented.

"Leo, you're in charge, and I need answers before the media starts some bullshit," the captain said.

"What else is new?" Bobby responded, slapping hands with another officer.

"Bobby, since you have a lot to say, you're first up for midnight patrol in the park."

"Captain, that's bullshit!" Bobby said.

"You want to make it for the rest of the week?"

"No, sir."

"Good. Grab a big cup of coffee because you'll need it, son." The captain slammed his folder closed and walked out of the room.

Leo followed him to his office.

"Shut the door," the captain said.

Leo clashed with the captain a few times, but he respected the work he put in to clean up the force in that station. His style mirrored his own, and that drew him to want to work alongside him. When he became a detective, Captain Samson was the first person who congratulated him.

"Tell me you have some type of idea."

"Captain, you know I hate to say this, but I think not only is it copycat, but we might find more bodies before we catch him."

"Shit, Leo."

"I didn't want to say anything in the room, but we need to increase it everywhere."

"You know how much that's going to cost."

"We don't want a repeat of Connor Little."

"I heard Jessica was here." The captain watched Leo's response.

"She is going to work my last nerve."

"You know how I feel about outsiders in police business."

"The chief likes her."

"At the end of the day, we have a case to solve. She needs to know if she messes anything up…"

"I'll explain it to her again."

"Please do."

"I was wondering about something else." Leo picked up the picture of the captain and his wife.

"What?"

"When are you going to retire?"

"Shit, if it's up to my wife, next month. But I plan to maybe in a year or two."

"See, married life is not all fun." Leo chuckled and put the picture back on the desk.

"Get out of my office before I call my wife and tell her you've been talking about her."

Leo held both hands up in surrender.

"Guy code, Captain."

"Not when you're married to my wife." They both laughed, and Leo left the office.

Leo shut the door and marched to his office when he heard a loud scream. He ran toward the front of the station and noticed three officers trying to wrestle a suspect to the ground.

"Bobby, if you can't handle him, maybe you need to find a new job." Leo gripped the suspect around the collar and shoved him toward the interrogation room.

"We had him," Bobby replied, unlocked the door, and secured the subject to a chair.

"What's your name?" Leo questioned him, and he snarled.

"Fuck you, cop!" He spat on the floor.

"We found him snooping around the location of the first victim."

"The club?"

"Yep. He was harassing some woman and wouldn't let her go."

"She owes me." The guy spat.

"He said he paid for sex, and she tried to skip out on him." Bobby shook his head.

"You hang out at the club often to solicit sex from women?" Leo stood in front of the table.

"I want a lawyer."

Leo slammed his hand on the table.

"We know you're the one killing those girls. You better confess now, and I might not go for death penalty."

"Aye, what the hell are you talking about?"

"The copycat killer," Bobby mentioned.

The suspect's eyes rose in surprise.

"Hold up, I haven't killed anyone. I might have slapped a few women, but I never killed them." His eyes pleaded.

"What do you think, Bobby?"

"He could be lying," Bobby answered.

Sweat broke out on his forehead.

"Please, man, I didn't hurt anybody. She can keep the money," he suggested.

"Keep him overnight so he can cool off." Leo explained, and Bobby nodded.

"This is bullshit! You don't have any evidence. I didn't kill those girls."

"Until we can confirm your story, you can hang out with us for the night." Leo stalked back to his office.

* * *

"YOU LOOK LIKE SHIT." Gilda poured coffee in his cup. Leo brushed his palm down his cheek.

"Long night of work."

"Where's your friend?"

"Who?"

"Jessica, you had breakfast with the other day."

"Gilda, I told you about minding your own business."

Gilda waved him off, leaning over the counter.

"Hush, you need a woman in your life so you can stop eating here."

"I like the food here."

"Me too, but a home-cooked meal would be better."

"Says the woman who doesn't cook for her husband." Leo watched Gilda giggle and put his plate in front of him. At least two nights out of the week, he came to the restaurant for dinner after a long night at the station. Once Bobby ran the rest of the story down, he ran a check on the suspect's name and found out he had a few warrants from drunk driving. It approached close to midnight when he left and stopped off to get food and see Gilda. Then he changed to sit and eat.

"Mind your business, Leo."

Gilda wiped the counter, then the menus.

"So, what case are you handling now?"

"The woman I brought here the other day?"

"Yeah."

"Her friend was one of the girls who was killed."

Gilda gasped.

"That poor child."

Leo thought the same way about Jessica. She never could catch a break, and she carried the weight of the world on her shoulders. He was at fault with her often but considered her a dear friend.

"She thinks someone is targeting her."

"How so?"

"You remember the women who were killed a year ago by Connor Little? It was all in the news."

"Of course. They played it on the news for days."

"Another one of her friends, Allison, was a victim."

"Leo, you can't be serious." Gilda froze.

"As a heart attack."

"She must really be confused."

"Many times, I tried to get her to take time off, but she refuses."

"She wants answers. I can understand that."

"Answers she probably can't handle."

"Women like that will find the answers with or without a man's help," Gilda explained.

"That's what I'm afraid of."

"Finish your food and go rest. You look like shit."

"Gilda, if only you were twenty years younger…"

"Boy, you couldn't handle a woman like me when I was your age, so spare me the flattery," Gilda teased and walked to another customer at the counter. Then he glanced through his call log from earlier in the day and saw Jessica's number multiple times. It was his fault that the conversation was cut off, and he planned to make amends.

"Hopefully, she listens to me."

While eating his steak, Leo watched reruns of his favorite baseball game on the television.

CHAPTER 9

"Hi, Jess."

"How are the kids, Lainey?" Jessica clicked through archives.

"Outside playing with their father."

"Tell them Aunt Jess says hello."

"What have you been up to lately? Saw the reports of another victim."

"They wouldn't let me talk to her, and the police are keeping things under wraps."

"Have you thought about coming back here?"

"Maybe a visit, but I love New York, Lainey." Jessica paused on the barn from her hometown and zoomed in on the statements from the kids in the area.

"I could come for a visit to see if I like New York."

"You don't need to do that."

"Our parents could watch the kids."

"Once they find the killer, we can plan a girls' trip."

"I thought you were going to stay away from the investigation."

"After the third victim, no way I could leave it alone."

"Are you seeing anyone?"

Lainey changed the subject.

"When would I have time, Lainey?"

"You have to make time to live your life, girl," Lainey joked.

"Yes, ma'am."

"Okay, don't make me sound like my mom."

"I bet you love the PTA and everything," Jessica teased.

"As a matter of fact. I'm the president."

"Oooh. Next you'll be the president of the board."

"Funny, but where are you?"

"At the library."

"I can already guess what you're doing."

"Then don't ask."

Jessica hated when people doubted her abilities and strength.

Lainey paused before she continued.

"Promise you'll be careful."

"Pinky promise."

"Let me find out why my child is screaming at the top of his lungs."

"Bye, Lainey."

"Bye, Jess." Lainey disconnected the call.

In her chair, Jessica scrolled through story after story about bodies that had been buried at the barn, up to the latest killings in New York. Although experts concluded it was an open and closed case, Jessica saw too many similarities and wished to expose the copycats and maybe even lead them to justice.

Ring!

"Hello, this is Jessica Smith."

"Hello, Jessica, this is Hilary, assistant to Dr. Richards. We have an opening right now if you want to come to speak with Dr Richards."

"Thank you very much. On my way."

Jessica closed out of the computer and headed to the coroner's office.

* * *

"Dr. Richards, thank you so much for meeting with me."

"Not every day do you get a story possibly written about you."

Jessica smiled and felt bad that she had lied about her reason for wanting to meet.

"You have a lovely office." Jessica peered at the family pictures on the wall.

"Thank you. My wife and kids bring me so much joy."

"I bet they do."

"So, should we get started on the interview?"

"Uhm… yes. But first, I wanted to get a feel for your work and talk about the realities of having to see dead bodies every day."

"My job is not for the weak stomach type of person." He pulled out the chair for her to sit.

"Thank you. Can you explain further?"

"As a reporter, you know what we have to face and come across. It makes you want to go into a dark place."

"I see what you're saying."

"You wouldn't believe the amount of times I've had to tell parents to ID loved ones."

"That has to be tough."

"I think to myself you need to stop because you can't go home to your own family and not be affected."

"Well, with a wife and young daughter, these serial killings have to be alarming," Jessica suggested.

"Two young girls were killed in the same way."

"Tragic, and I hear without a trace of DNA."

"The third victim hasn't woken up, so they haven't determined if it's connected."

"I see."

"Do you need to take pictures of me for the article?"

"I'll let the photographer come back and take pictures of you." Jessica took out her phone and turned on the recorder.

"Sounds good to me. Where should we start?"

"What made you get into this line of work?"

"That's a long story."

"I have time." Jessica smiled, and he described how he changed the course of work in college, to meeting his future wife, and present day. Hours later, Jessica was back in the office to type up her notes on the doctor and make arrangements to have a photographer go back to get pictures. She would pitch the story to her editor to get him off her back since she'd avoided him for the past few days. Even though it was a sad situation, her editor didn't care beyond turning in the assigned stories. As she bit her lip and propped her arm on the desk, she stared at the screen. The only conclusion she could figure out was that the person was able to lure all the women away. Most times, unless you were in a position of authority, a woman wouldn't automatically go along with a regular guy without a fight.

"A cop."

All the lights went out in the building. The hairs on the back of her neck rose, as she squinted at the clock on her desk.

"Ugh. It shouldn't be cut off now." Normally, the office lights would go off at eleven, and it was only eight at night. Jessica rose out of her seat and went to knock on the door next to her when she saw it was closed.

"Everyone's already left."

Bang!

She jumped back against the door in fear at a loud noise.

"Who's there? Lonnie, are you still here!" Jessica yelled and looked toward the breakroom. Lonnie was a part of the cleaning crew that worked some nights when Jessica stayed late; they'd forged a great friendship.

Bang!

"Arghh! Okay, get yourself together. It's probably a mouse or something." Jessica slowly strolled toward the breakroom to see where the noise was when the lights came back on.

"Lonnie! Lonnie!" Jessica looked around the empty breakroom.

She blew out a breath and turned to go back to her office. Once she shut the door, the lights turned back off, and she picked the phone up to make a call.

"Hello, Hello… It's dead," she muttered aloud, then scanned the room. She reached to grab her coat, purse, and cell to try to reach the editor. After she locked her office door, she jogged to the elevator and hit the button for the main floor. Not responding, she gave up and went toward the stairs. Then the editor picked up.

"Jessica, this better be good."

"I'm at the office, and the lights went off."

"Okay."

"You know they usually don't turn off until after ten."

"Well, maybe they ran a test or something."

"So, why is the office line dead?"

"Jessica, have you been drinking?"

Jessica ran down the stairs when she heard a door slam a few floors up from her.

"I think someone is following me."

"How can you be sure?"

"Everyone left already. I called out for Lonnie when the lights went out." Jessica shoved the door open.

"Argghhh!"

"Jessica! Jessica!" Ellen the editor screamed through the phone.

"I'm sorry, lady. Don't call the cops." He stammered back and forth.

Jessica held her chest to catch her breath.

"Jessica! Can you hear me?"

"Oh my God! My phone." Jessica crawled beside him and grabbed her phone that fell.

"Yeah, I'm here."

"What happened?"

"I came out of the back entrance and bumped into a homeless man."

"Go home and get some rest."

"I think someone chased me out of the building."

"We'll talk about it later."

"All right."

"Get home safe."

"I will." Jessica closed her eyes and unclenched her fist to calm her breathing.

She contemplated on whether it would cause a bigger issue if she called Leo to check out the building but decided to just head home and sleep off the day. Before she walked away, she looked back at the building, and all of the lights came back on. Then she glanced through the window and saw the elevator ding.

"Someone set this up." She released a breath.

CHAPTER 10

The next morning, Jessica turned the shower off, grabbed a towel to wrap around her body, and stood in front of the steamed mirror. Her hair was damp and curly after she conditioned and shampooed. One of her plans was to make an appointment with the hairstylist, but each time she tried, something else got in the way. She shuffled to the bedroom and removed a pair of jeans and shirt to place on her bed.

Ring!

Ring!

"Too early for drama." But she reluctantly sat on the bed and answered her cell.

"I wanted to check in on you after last night."

"Bianca?"

"Yes."

"What do you mean about last night?"

"Well, the other night at the hospital."

"Oh, yeah. I'm fine."

"We didn't get a chance to catch up, and I was slammed."

"I figured."

"I haven't forgotten about our dinner."

"I know, sorry. Work is just crowding my brain."

"Understandable, you have an important job. We can do stuff besides dinner."

"Thanks. I'll keep you updated. How are you doing?"

"Surprisingly fine. I started to talk with a therapist."

"My family says I should seek out therapy."

"It's helped me so much. You'd be surprised what clarity you'll find."

"Maybe you can recommend your doctor," Jessica joked.

"Hey, it never hurts."

They both giggled.

"True but let me finish getting dressed for my day, and I'll call you to figure out the plans."

"Don't be a stranger."

"Never. Talk soon."

"Soon, my friend."

"Bye."

Jessica slipped her bra and panties on, then reached for the jeans and shirt.

Knock! Knock!

"I'm popular today." She sauntered out of the bedroom to the front door, looked through the peephole, and smiled.

"What do I owe for this visit?" Leo held a bag up with two cups in his hand.

"I hadn't heard from you and wanted to check in before I got slammed with work."

Jessica grabbed the bag and coffee out of his hand.

"Mmmm… my favorite… chai latte."

"Cost me almost six bucks."

"You know I love my expensive drinks." Leo opened the bag and dug out a croissant. Jessica removed a donut.

"Next round is on me."

"Did I interrupt you?"

Jessica shook her head.

"I was about to leave to meet you actually."

"What for?"

"Last night at my job, all the lights went out."

"And?"

"Here me out."

Leo wiped his hands with the napkin.

"Jess, it sounds like a normal building function."

"The hours are automatic and cut off later than eight. Plus, there was the banging noise."

"Like your boss said, maybe a rat or something got in the building."

"You think I'm crazy, don't you?"

"I mean…"

"Ugh… Whatever, Leo."

"There is no way it just happened to be timed after I went to the library and looked into the barn."

Leo stopped eating.

"You did what?"

"I went to look into more deaths at the barn."

He dropped the croissant on the table and groaned.

"Are you trying to get me fired?"

"No, I want you to understand how things are connected."

"It won't matter if you end up in jail for tampering with a case."

"Thanks for the support, Leo."

Leo jumped up.

"Listen, I need to get going. Please try to stay out of trouble."

"Sure will, Mr. Detective."

Leo opened the door and turned to look back at her. The disapproval in his stare caught Jessica's eye.

* * *

HE SAT outside her building in his car and listened to his favorite motivational speaker talk about how he could better himself and live up to God's plans. His cravings intensified and almost cost him last night when he showed up at her job and watched her while she worked. The last employee had left, and he slipped through unnoticed with an employee badge. He was close enough that he could smell her perfume when she went to the breakroom. At work, he counted down the time he could get a glimpse of her and be alone, but the homeless man made him retreat.

"Asshole." He slapped the steering wheel and started his car up when he saw Leo come out of her building. Her type of man was like Leo Walsh, and he couldn't compete unless he made a drastic decision only at the perfect time. He trailed Leo out of the building structure and on the main road to keep a distance. Today, he was supposed to find a new girl, but he wanted to spend time tracking Leo's movements and then get back to Jessica. He knew she wouldn't work late tonight after the day prior. More than likely, she'd try to meet up with Leo or do more checking into the girl at the hospital. That was a loose end he planned to take care of when he felt it was clear. Some police were out front, and it would raise suspicion if he made contact too early.

"Show me what you're about, Mr. Walsh."

Leo turned up at the park of the third victim.

"He won't find anything."

He smirked and removed a cigarette from the glove

compartment. He turned the radio on and watched Leo speak with officers outside the bathroom.

"*Still no word on the woman who was found in the park unconscious*," a reporter explained.

"Good." He laughed.

"*Such a tragic thing to happen. We have to believe the person behind this will turn themselves into the police*," the reporter said.

"*Kathy, all we can do is pray for the other two victims and hope someone catches the person behind this tragedy.*"

"*You're right, Tony. The police of captain ordered an around-the-clock increase in police presence*," the reporter commented.

"*People like that will slip up and make a mistake.*"

"Fuck you!" he yelled, slammed his hand on the window, and laughed.

"We ask everyone to stay on the lookout and send your prayers to the young woman in the hospital," the reporter pleaded.

He turned the radio off and drove off.

"Take care of my little problem now," he stated.

CHAPTER 11

The air in the building went still as she looked around the area, eased the hairpin to pop the lock, slid through the door, and turned her flashlight off.

"Focus, Jessica." She walked over to an empty table; the books were all on the shelf neatly lined up. Jessica went down the hallway to the bedroom, opening the door only to find the room had been cleaned. In the closet, she found clothes still hung up. Her hope to find some clues had dried up. Sifting through the clothes rack, she squatted down to the ground, and nothing stood out. Her brows dipped in frustration, as she whirled around to check the drawers and blew out a breath.

"Nothing."

Her last hope was to speak with the woman they saved from the park. A moment passed, and she walked out of the room and back to the living room with the door open.

"What are you doing here?" an older woman spoke.

"I'm sorry."

"Do you live in the building?"

Jessica cleared her throat. This would only put her in a

bad situation with the police if she called them, and Leo found out.

"Uhhh, I actually work with the newspaper. I was doing a story on the murders."

"You shouldn't be here."

"Are you the owner of the building?"

"I live here, and I know the police wouldn't want someone prying around here."

"You're right. I just want to make sure we catch the person."

"Please just leave."

"Sorry to disturb you." Jessica walked around her and left the apartment, removing her phone to send a text to Leo when a message popped up.

Bianca: You're coming out with me.

Jessica: I can't tonight.

Bianca: Not taking no for an answer.

Jessica: Where?

Bianca: A club I like.

Jessica: All right. Let me go home and change.

Putting the key in the lock, she opened the door and slipped the phone back into her pocket. As she climbed into the car after throwing her bag in the back, she held onto her thoughts as she turned the ignition. She'd have an evening with Bianca for the sake of clearing her mind, then she would contact Leo and talk over her weird thoughts with him, and maybe talk to the girl in the hospital.

* * *

JESSICA STOOD in front of the mirror, applied blush on her cheeks, and picked up her favorite plum lipstick for another coat.

Ring!

Jessica tossed her hair and answered the phone on FaceTime.

"Leo, did you get my message?"

"You're dressed up fancy."

"Bianca invited me to go out with her." Jessica ran a comb through her hair.

"I did get your message. I think it would be crazy for anyone in law enforcement."

Jessica lifted her phone, stepped out of the bathroom, and turned off the light. She headed to the living room, and grabbed her jacket, keys, and purse.

"I know the old boys club makes it seem impossible but think about it, Leo."

"Jess, you're too close."

Jessica shut and locked the door behind her and strolled to the elevator.

"Maybe you don't want to see the truth."

"Where are you going?"

"My phone might cut off... about to get on the elevator."

"Try not to get too wasted."

Jessica rolled her eyes and ended the call. A few minutes later, she climbed in her car to drive toward the club and sent a message to Bianca.

Jessica: On my way!

Bianca: See you soon, babe.

Thirty minutes later, she parked in front of the valet.

"I'm meeting someone here."

"Here you go." He extended a ticket and took her keys.

"Thank you." Jessica's heels clicked against the gravel as she trekked to the guard, and he removed the barrier to allow her entrance.

Loud music blasted throughout as Jessica glanced around the vibrant room with a variety of lights. The DJ spoke over the microphone to keep the crowd going on the dance floor.

She shifted from one foot to the other and noticed Bianca in the corner with her hand up.

"This place is huge." Jessica removed her jacket and set it down next to her on the empty chair.

"It really is, right?" Bianca sipped on her martini.

"How many have you had?" Jessica pointed at the martini.

"First one. I planned on finding someone to take home."

"Oooh, do tell." Jessica cupped her chin and crossed her legs.

"There are so many cute guys here." Bianca motioned around the large, open room. The place was bigger than the last club she visited with her best friend.

"I thought you'd bring more friends with you."

The waitress approached their booth.

"Hi, I'm Kimmi. What can I get you to drink?" the bottle girl questioned

"I'll have what she's having."

"A dirty martini." Bianca tapped her glass.

"Coming right up, ladies."

A crowd of women gathered on the floor to dance. Strobe lights changed from red to blue. A wall splashed a live feed of women dancing.

"Here you go, ladies." Kimmi held out two more drinks.

"Thank you." Jessica picked up her glass and took a gulp.

"So, tell me how the case is going. Have the police made a break?"

"No, not yet, and it's frustrating." Jessica slammed the rest of her drink down.

"I mean they should have a man arrested by now."

"Well, the good thing is that the one girl was found."

Bianca's eyes rose as she placed her drink on the table.

"I forgot to tell you." Jessica kept her gaze. "She didn't make it."

Jessica gasped.

"Wait! Bianca, you're kidding me, right?"

Bianca's eyes flickered to the waitress when she brought two more drinks.

"I can't get too personal, but she didn't make it that night."

"I need to go to the restroom." Jessica stood and pressed her hand against her cheek.

"I didn't want to worry you." Bianca started to stand.

"No, I'll be fine. Let me run to the restroom." Jessica ran to the back hallway to the bathroom.

Jessica looked at herself in the bathroom mirror. She had all her questions ready for the woman found in the park. There was a high probability that it was a member of the police force. She turned on the faucet and grabbed the napkin to clean herself up.

"I need to talk to Leo," she muttered, pulling her phone out to make a call when the door burst open, and a group of girls came in laughing. She tucked it back in her purse in a rush and went back to the booth.

"Are you okay? I was worried." Bianca extended her hand on top of her palm.

"Need to drink this news away."

"Same, this is just nerve wracking." Bianca lifted the glass and handed Jessica her drink.

"After this, we go dancing on the floor."

"Cheers to that." Bianca winked her eye and smiled at Jessica.

Jessica closed her eyes, taking in the alcohol. The warm sensation was overwhelming, and she took another sip, but then she felt light-headed.

"You gulped that down." Bianca giggled.

"I didn't know I needed that, but I'm getting another one."

"Tonight's on me. Anything you want." The girls clinked glasses again.

CHAPTER 12

$\mathcal{A}$ huge headache subsided, and her memories of the night faded in and out, so she tried to sit up but felt restraints on her hands. Her eyes flickered open, and a startled expression crossed her face.

"Where am I?" She looked from her left to right in an empty bedroom.

Despite Jessica's groans and her attempts to yank her arm, nothing moved. She noticed handcuffs on her arms and legs. Eventually, she noticed she wore only a bra and panties.

"Help!" Jessica screamed.

Jessica yanked harder on her wrists.

"Please! Help me."

The door opened and relief came over her.

"Thank God. Bianca help me."

Bianca's face held no emotion. She stalked over to the bed and sat by her side and raised her hand to her cheek.

"Shushhhh."

"Hurry up before he comes back," Jessica rambled on.

Bianca smiled.

"Jessica, you've been determined, I must give you that."

"What? We can talk after we get out of here." Jessica tossed her head back and forth.

"Sorry, Jessica, you're not leaving."

"Bianca, you have—" Realization sank in. In that moment that Bianca smiled, lifted her hand, and rubbed her cheek.

"It was you."

"Bingo."

"Bianca, you killed Marnie."

"Well, I had some help."

As she heard footsteps, she glanced over Bianca's shoulder to see Kian standing in the doorway.

"Ki-Kian," she stuttered.

"Jessica."

Bianca reached out and grabbed Kian's hand.

"We've been waiting to bring you here."

"Where are we?"

"Home." Bianca whirled around and kissed Kian on the lips.

"You killed Marnie."

Kian released Bianca and bit his bottom lip.

"Marnie didn't realize what was happening."

"Please let me go."

Kian's eyes darkened.

"We're just getting started."

Bianca walked out of the room, and Kian stepped closer to Jessica.

"No! Stay away from me!" she screamed.

Kian slipped a pair of keys from his pocket.

"No need to be scared, princess," Kian taunted and ran a hand up her thigh.

"Kian, please, you don't want to do this."

Kian grunted.

Under his touch, Jessica squirmed and eyed him.

"Kian, remove the cuffs on her legs." Bianca walked back in the room.

"Kian, please! You know me." She drew back.

Bianca dropped a bag on the floor.

Jessica prayed Leo would find her.

Immediately after her legs were freed, she tried to kick and get out of his hold.

"Aye! Stop moving, or you're going to stay locked in this position," Bianca shouted and pointed her finger in Jessica's face.

"Bianca! Bianca! No." Jessica screamed, and Bianca moved a needle toward her arm.

Darkness pulled over her eyes.

"Leo... Leo," Jessica whispered.

She regretted not taking Leo's advice to stop looking into what happened to Marnie and the other women. This was the second time her life was in danger, and no one could find her or know that she was even missing. Jessica's world became a complete shambles again, and she ran out of ways to save herself. A single tear fell on her cheek, and her head slumped forward. At this moment, Kian wanted to finally take his chance with Jessica, but Bianca was in the room. Usually, she'd be fine with a third party in the relationship, and both would have fun with the person they picked for the night. Bianca was just as interested in Jessica for herself and didn't want to leave them alone. Kian took it to mean that she wanted to have first go with Jessica. Bianca put the needle back in her bag and rubbed Jessica's leg.

"She's sweet and calm like this, baby," Kian said. Bianca leaned on Kian's back and rubbed the top of his head.

"Let her rest for the night. Maybe we can try tomorrow."

"What are we going to do?"

"We'll have a little fun with her first before we take the next step."

"Did you cover yourself at the club?" Kian wrapped a hand around her waist.

Bianca stood on tiptoes to kiss him on the lips.

"I have to get back to the station," Kian reminded her, and Bianca nodded.

"Hurry up and clear out anything you have at the station."

"Did you get the tickets for our flights?"

"I paid in cash, and we will fly out tomorrow night."

"Great, that gives me enough time to wrap up any last-minute situations," Kian said and bent down to press a kiss on Jessica's forehead.

"Remember what I said—don't stop off besides the station."

"I know, baby." He rubbed her back.

Bianca gripped his chin.

"If you follow my plan, we can be gone soon and find someone new."

"Why not take her with us?"

Bianca slapped him across the face.

"Do you want her for yourself? Is that it!" Bianca yelled.

"Bianca, calm down."

"Get out of my face."

Kian shifted around and bent down to pick up the bag to leave her alone.

"She's temptation," Bianca mumbled.

* * *

JESSICA GROANED hours later and felt wetness on her chest as her eyes opened slowly. To her right, she saw a tray with a sandwich, fruit, and a bottle of water.

"No! Get off me." Jessica tried to shift out of her grip.

Bianca moved the towel from Jessica's chest over to her arm.

"I need you clean before we have fun." Bianca gleamed and tossed a towel in the bowl.

"Bianca, you need to let me go."

"Now, why should I let my favorite doll leave me?"

"You're crazy."

Bianca cackled.

"Can I confess something to you, Jessica?"

"Why did you kill Marnie?"

"Marnie was a trial run for us."

"She didn't deserve what you did."

"See that's how I know you don't understand me."

"You're a monster!"

"Monster, you don't mean it, Jess." Bianca removed the top from a bottle of water.

"Tell me the truth, is Kian threatening you?"

"Would you like some water?"

"I want to go home!"

"I'm tired of your begging."

"Okay, okay. Just let me use the bathroom."

"No."

"Can I have something to eat please?"

"I'll feed you."

"Bianca, I can feed myself."

"Promise you won't do anything stupid?"

"Where can I go? My legs are strapped to the bed."

Bianca leaned forward and unlocked her hands. Jessica rubbed her wrists, and Bianca moved the tray over her lap so that Jessica could pick up the sandwich and take a bite.

"Sorry it's not what you're used to, but we don't have enough time." Bianca reached her hand out to grab a piece of fruit when Jessica slammed the sandwich in Bianca's face.

"Bitch!" Bianca shouted. Jessica grabbed the plate and hit Bianca over the head.

"You're insane!" Jessica continued to hit Bianca over her head until she stopped moving. Quickly, she grabbed the key from her hand and unlocked her feet. Hurriedly, she climbed out of the bed and fell on the ground from no circulation in her legs.

"Fuck." Jessica crawled and reached for her clothes on top of the chair. Slowly, she rubbed her legs and then jumped up, found her shoes, and ran out of the room in search for a phone.

"I need Leo." Jessica ran down the hallway to the living room and saw she was in an unfamiliar place. She grabbed the door and felt a hand on the back of her hair.

"Get back here!"

"Arghhh!"

Bianca yanked her to the floor.

"Let me go!" Upon being punched in the head by Jessica, Bianca fell to her side. Jessica scrambled to her feet, raced toward the door, jerked it open, and exited the building.

CHAPTER 13

"*L*eo, here's the sketches."

Judy marched in his office and tossed the folder to him.

"Did you look at them yet?"

"Nope, they said you wanted them immediately."

"Thanks, Judy. Did they get anything else out of the girl?"

"Should be in the transcript."

"All right."

When the young woman was interviewed before she died, Leo noticed that she gave the description of a police badge. Curious, he flipped through other papers and saw a sketch of a woman.

"I woke up to a woman and man, and me in chains," Leo read from the statement. Everything in front of him made his ears perk up. In the corner of his eye, he noticed Kian walk past after he pulled up the photo of the young man. His gut churned as he glanced at the picture again.

"Son of a bitch." Leo slammed the folder shut, grabbed his badge, gun, and keys, and slowly stood. He stared at

Kian in surprise. There was a box in his hands and a jacket slung over his shoulders.

"Judy, I need you to keep this quiet and put some people on Kian's home."

"Kian Young? What for?" Judy lifted the receiver.

"I have a gut feeling he's the copycat killer."

"Shit, Leo, that's a big assumption."

"If I'm lying, I'll bet my pension on it then."

"Tell the chief now."

"Keep it quiet between a few people. I'm going to follow him."

"He said today was his last day."

"That's a big red flag." Leo hurried out of the station to maintain a safe distance when he saw him close the car door. Leo jogged to his car and trailed him when he turned right at the light. When he pulled into some apartments that didn't match his, he watched. Two cars over, he parked, then jumped out of his car and followed Kian, who dropped his box and turned to face him with a gun.

"You should have left it alone, Leo."

"Drop the gun, Kian."

Kian chuckled.

"She's already dead."

"Who's dead?"

"Jessica."

Leo moved forward, and Kian smirked.

"You come near me, and I'll shoot."

"Too late, Kian. I can help you avoid a life sentence."

"They needed to die."

"Why, Kian?"

Leo slowly shifted forward.

"Because they tried to act like I didn't matter. Bianca showed me differently."

"Bianca." Leo remembered the name of the woman who worked with Marnie at the hospital.

"My girlfriend."

"Kian, put the gun down."

"Kian!" a familiar voice shouted, and Kian started to turn around when something sharp went over his head and knocked him down.

"Jessica!" Leo ran toward her, and police sirens grew louder as they approached.

Jessica wrapped her arms around Leo.

"Jessica, are you all right?" Leo rubbed her back.

"Leo, they tried to kill me," Jessica cried. Leo directed a few officers to check on Kian.

"What happened?"

"I just remember going to the club, then I woke up chained to a bed here."

"Where's Bianca?"

"In the apartment. I knocked her over the head." Jessica refused to let Leo out of her sight.

"He has a pulse. We'll take him down," an officer relayed.

"Which apartment, Jess?" Leo rubbed his finger over the bruise on her eye.

"Upstairs on the right." Jessica motioned to the stairs.

"Stay here with them, and I'll be right back."

"No, please don't leave me, Leo."

"Okay. You guys go check and make sure you rope off the scene," he ordered.

"I almost died."

Leo walked her to the ambulance. They checked her vitals as he held her hand.

"Did they touch you? What went on in the apartment?"

"Hard to explain. I just want to go home."

"Do you want my men to drive you or take you to hospital?"

"No, I want to go with you."

"Jess." She was frightened and shocked beyond words. Leo relaxed his shoulders as he sighed. Being saved twice and never speaking with a therapist meant she would try to sweep this incident under the rug.

"Give me a second to make sure everything is wrapped up here."

"Leo."

"Yeah?"

"Thank you."

* * *

"Breaking news has come to light that the copycat killer was a police officer and nurse," a reporter provided live commentary. Jessica occupied the deck of Leo's apartment, scrolling through her cell phone. After what felt like an endless night of officers taking her statement, the hospital decided she should be kept overnight in case she had a concussion. Finally, Leo decided to put an end to the night and drove her back to his place so she could take a hot bath and sleep in a proper bed. He had been on the phone with the police chief all morning and wanted police officers outside his house to avoid reporters. Yesterday, when a food delivery arrived at his place, a few people tried to take pictures from inside. There were pictures of Jessica, Kian, and Bianca throughout the day, and there were claims that Kian should not have been allowed on the force after reports that he was inappropriate with some inmates. The moment Leo held up a plate of food, Jessica closed the video, and started to scroll through her messages.

"Are you hungry?"

"Not really."

Leo placed the food on the table and sat opposite her.

"I know it might sound stupid to ask if you slept last night."

"Probably got a good hour of sleep."

"The chief is going to keep a few officers outside while you're here."

"Sorry for imposing on your space."

"You never have to apologize to me."

Jessica caught Leo's stare.

"News reporters probably won't leave your house for a while."

"Are you saying you'll be here a while?"

Jessica chuckled.

"You don't seem like the type to have roommates."

"I don't, but I'll make an exception for you."

"Leo, are you being nice to me?"

"Don't tell anybody."

Both of them laughed.

"He had me fooled," Leo said.

"Who?"

"Kian. I thought I knew him. The whole thing has me side-eyeing everybody."

"Bianca had me fooled. I thought she was a friend. Can't even imagine what Marnie went through."

Jessica covered her face and cried. Leo knelt in front of her and wrapped his arms around her shoulders.

"Shushhh… Jess, you can't blame yourself."

"I'm cursed, Leo. Why is this happening to my life?"

"You're not cursed; the world has crazy people."

"All of my friends are targeted."

"I never want to hear you talk like this again. You are amazing and didn't warrant any of this from Bianca and Kian."

"I know you're right, but my heart and head aren't synced."

"Maybe take a break from the newspaper and go away somewhere?"

"I'm too afraid to leave."

"Then I'll go with you."

"You can't just up and leave."

"I'm a detective, Jess. If you need time away, as your friend, I'm the one to make it happen."

"You'll do that for me?"

Leo lifted her chin.

"Thanks, Leo."

"First thing you should do is eat and then get some rest."

Jessica picked up the plate of bacon, eggs, and pancakes and started to eat.

"Maybe I'll hire you to be my personal bodyguard."

"Now that'll be a major story. Detective hired as personal guard for news reporter." Leo and Jessica burst into laughter.

"I can't beat the pension and vacation hours though."

"Probably not." Leo picked up a piece of bacon from her plate. Jessica slapped his hand.

"Get your own food. That's my bacon."

"Really, Jess."

"What? I'm hungry."

A chuckle escaped Leo's lips as he stood and went back inside. The way he looked at her when she returned the bacon made Jessica smile. They'd become great friends, and she was glad to laugh after suffering a terrible experience. To escape the chaos that would continue while they worked out the charges, a vacation from the city would be refreshing. Suddenly, a wind blew, and Jessica was reminded of Marnie and Allison together and maintained their memory by looking down at her and Lainey.

"I promise," Jessica muttered, looking up in the sky.

* * *

I HOPE you enjoyed Jessica's story so far. Please also check out "**Mirror of Danger (A Jessica Smith Mystery) Book 3**" **coming soon.** Also, if you love thrillers, mystery, and suspense, check out **Agent Red: Fatal Memory Book 1 here.** Another thriller, crime fiction "**Ruined**" **here**

Check out free short here *"The Firm"* https://payhip.com/b/py7S

Grab Boxset "**Agent Red 1-3**" here https://payhip.com/b/1KcxY

SNEAK PEEK

MIRROR OF DANGER (A JESSICA SMITH BOOK 3)

Jessica thought she'd seen the worst of death; the tragedies in her life almost had her defeated. But things only get worst as she goes from local reporter to national news. More prominent cases start to her desk, and Leo has no choice but to help her solve a new crime that puts them in danger with a more significant threat they've never seen coming.

READING ORDER OF MIRROR SERIES

Mirror of Lies Book 1
https://books2read.com/u/mgjEPx
Mirror of Lust Book 2
https://books2read.com/u/mVRpz2
Mirror of Danger Book 3
Mirror of Murder Book 4

READING ORDER OF AGENT RED SERIES

1. **Agent Red: Fatal Memory Book**
   https://books2read.com/u/4j2PYX
2. **Agent Red-Fatal Target Book**
   https://books2read.com/u/bWP8Jq
3. **Agent Red-Fatal Crime Book**
   https://books2read.com/u/mZadZJ
4. **Agent Red-Fatal Justice Book**
   https://books2read.com/u/mq07wd
5. **Agent Red-Fatal Enemy Book**
   https://books2read.com/u/bxe01q
6. **Agent Red-Fatal Death Book**
   https://books2read.com/u/mqwlRv

WHAT'S NEXT?

Want to know what happens next? Follow me at the links below to catch the next release.

Thank you so much for reading, and if you enjoyed the crazy ride and decided to leave a review, we'd truly appreciate the support. Reviews are the lifeblood of the publishing world. They're read, appreciated, and needed. Please consider taking the time to leave a few words on Goodreads or BookBub.

Sign up for updates and sneak peeks at the sites below:
www.authoravasking.com

ACKNOWLEDGMENTS

I want to thank my team, who helps me behind the scenes, from my editors to my test readers and graphic designers, and the list goes on. I truly appreciate each of you for keeping me on my toes.

ABOUT THE AUTHOR

Ava S. King is the debut author of thriller, mystery, suspense, and psychological crime novels.

If you want to know when the next book will come out, please visit Author Ava S. King website at http://www.authoravasking.com, where you can sign up to receive an email for her next release.

* 9 7 8 1 9 5 5 2 3 3 2 3 1 *